Fairy
Cookbook

Home Sweet Home

A Little Book of Fairy Dwellings

Based on the Original Flower Fairies™ Books
by Cicely Mary Barker

Frederick Warne

Dear Friend,

What does home mean to you?
A place you go to every day?
A house filled with the people you love?
A shelter? Or just the nicest place to be?
To a Flower Fairy home means
wherever the flowers grow, be it
in a meadow or a forest, by a stream,
or in your garden. Our fairy
neighbourhood stretches farther than
the eye can see and all fairies inside it
are considered friends.

Perhaps your home is made of bricks,
wood, or maybe even ice! Every inch of a
Flower Fairy's home is built with natural
materials – the things we find all around us.
We can be very inventive and love making
fairy furniture and household items.

Finding out about our homes
will bring you one step closer
to the Flower Fairies.
Take a look inside... we're
waiting to say 'Welcome!'

Love,
The Flower Fairies

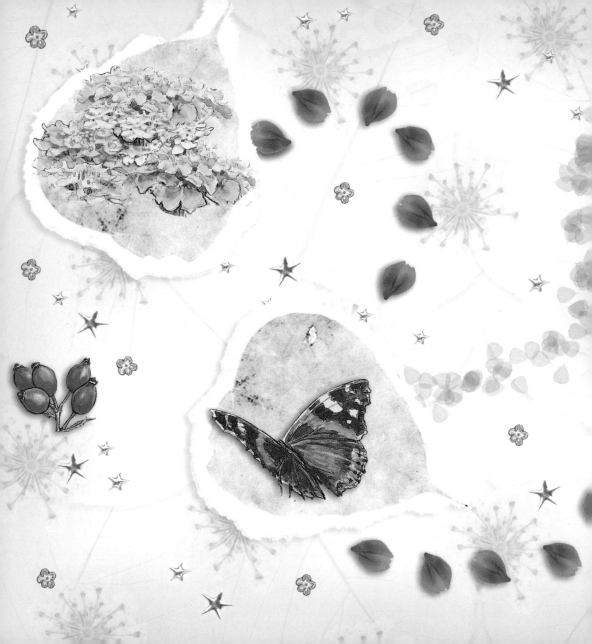

Fairy Places

Where We Live

Flower Fairies live in all sorts of different places. From sun-soaked meadows to woodland hollows, and river banks to well-tended flower beds – if you're lucky you may be able to spot a Flower Fairy wherever flowers, plants and trees grow!

Rush-Grass and Cotton-Grass live in wild, untamed places such as moorland and marshes.

Beautiful flowerbeds are home to the garden Flower Fairies. The Phlox Fairy loves to sing and dance amongst her white and pink blooms!

Some Flower Fairies, like Willow, live by clear blue streams or shady pools. It's peaceful by the water's edge, so she has lots of time to polish her leaves and play with her friends!

Acorn lives high up in the branches of the oak tree. Woodland glades and leafy hollows are home to many of the tree Flower Fairies.

In springtime, if you look carefully, you can spot Blackthorn's pretty flowers peeking through hedges and bushes.

Taking a Trip

Fairies love to travel to visit friends and
relatives, or to find tasty things to eat.
There are thousands of tiny trails they can
follow, but sometimes it's more fun to catch
a lift! There are lots of ways to travel in
Flower Fairyland!

After heavy rain, fairies don't want
to get their feet wet. It's fun to get a
ride on a friendly grasshopper.

Tree fairies like Silver Birch get around
easily by swinging from tree to tree.

LILY POND
5 minutes
fast flying!

If you're going a long way or have a baby with you, there are special places you can wait for passing birds, to hitch a lift.

All Flower Fairies need to know where they're going!
Forgetful fairies carry petals to drop along the way so they can find their way back home.

Even fairies must have a ticket to travel.

1 TICKET
to
the Old Oak T...

Thinking Spots

Fairy places are always bustling, but everyone needs a quiet place to be alone once in a while. The Flower Fairies have four special thinking spots: the Elm tree at the edge of the meadow, a patch of Candytuft in the flowerbed, the Forget-Me-Nots in the wood, and the Rose Hips in the hedges. What sort of thinking might a Flower Fairy do?

The little patch of Candytuft in the rockery is the perfect place to decide what to give Tulip for her birthday.

The big Elm tree provides a perfect, private thinking spot.

"I hope Buttercup will dance with me at the ball."

There's lots of peace and quiet to be had by the Rose Hips.

"I wonder where I'll fly off to tomorrow?"

Forget-Me-Not has spent so long dreaming in her thinking spot, she's forgotten that it's way past lunchtime!

HOME
SWEET
HOME

Fairy
Havens

Take Shelter

Though the essence of a home comes from those who live in it, Flower Fairies are also very practical. Outdoor living is a fine thing, but you need to be prepared for all sorts of weather. Each season needs a different type of shelter.

In summer a big leaf is an ideal parasol when the sun gets too hot.

Primrose makes a pretty spring canopy that will protect little ones from a light shower.

Tree-top living is best in autumn,
when there are leaves all around
and the berries are plentiful.

No one could be more snug than a fairy in winter
surrounded by this silky fluff!

Desirable Designs

For tip-top advice on how to create
a home fit for a Flower Fairy,
we need look no further than
Dogwood, a fairy who knows just
how to make every home both
beautiful and comfortable.

Dogwood studied at the
famous Acorn Academy
of Floral Furnishings.

Little Clover needs
some help hanging
her new doorbell.

Toadflax knows that
Dogwood has very
good advice!

DOGWOOD
DESIGNS

Dogwood's Bazaar has a good supply of everything you might need, and he is always on hand with helpful tips and suggestions for every fairy!

Soft dandelions are perfect as chairs.

Twigs make good tent poles for camping trips.

A fuchsia flower makes a lovely doorbell (that only fairies can hear).

Make a soft carpet with petals and moss.

Big leaves are an excellent canopy.

Periwinkle is using a long stem to paint his room blue!

Crocus flowers make dramatic floor lights.

Fairy Furnishings

Delightful Dining

Fairy dining rooms are warm and welcoming, with plenty of room for friends. Fairies just love to feast, and there are always good reasons for celebrating!

An upturned Canterbury Bell makes an excellent dining table, with its stylish purple tablecloth.

Sturdy mushrooms are perfect stools for fairies.

Sitting Pretty

The fairies love to relax on a comfortable chair in the evening. Harebell's flower makes a very good lamp, if a kind glow-worm will oblige by sitting inside!

A Willow Catkin makes a good feather duster.

Mulberry used some seeds and leaves he collected to make this collage.

Although their natural surroundings are beautiful enough, Flower Fairies love to dabble in homemade art on winter evenings when it is too cold to be outside!

Sipping and Nibbling

Fairies love to host fabulous fairy feasts. Their kitchens and pantries are always filled with yummy ripe fruits and tasty crunchy nuts. In the summer time, the little Strawberry Fairy is very busy harvesting all his fruit. They are delicious to eat on their own, but if you were to visit the Strawberry Fairy during the summer, this is what he would offer you.

Fairy Cookbook

Strawberry's Secret Fairy Nectar

Blend together a handful of strawberries with a glass of orange juice, and a tablespoon each of yogurt and honey. Be sure to ask a grown-up fairy to help you use the blender.

Dishes and bowls.

Acorn and Horse-Chestnut bowls.

Fruit and nuts.

Cutlery.

Sycamore wings are used as serving spoons.

Fairy Nectar

The fairies search the gardens and meadows for cups and glasses.

At the end of every fabulous feast, there's lots of cleaning up to do!

Just what you need for scrubbing out that pan!

A Hazel Catkin is used as a washing-up brush.

Blissful Bedrooms

Wardrobes

To ensure the most delightful dreams, bedroom furniture must be comfy and warm enough for the most delicate fairy.

Spindleberry Rack: for hanging clothes and hats.

Beds & Bedding

Fluffy: a comfy pillow made of Poplar.

Snug: a silky blanket made of Cotton-grass.

Slumber Leaf: a perfect hammock made from the leaf of a Sweet Chestnut tree.

Nursery

Changing Seat: to prevent babies from wriggling around when we're trying to dress them!

Moss Mat: babies learn to crawl on velvety moss to protect their knees.

Caring Cradle: the leaves of a Forget-Me-Not keep fairy babies happy.

Each Flower Fairy decorates their bedroom using their favourite colours!

FREDERICK WARNE

Published by the Penguin Group
Penguin Books Ltd, 80 Strand, London WC2R 0RL, England
New York, Australia, Canada, India, New Zealand, South Africa

ISBN 0 7232 5381 1

Printed in China

DOGWOOD
DESIGNS